I0788383

Who is Grandma?

Written by Nikolina Plotinskiy

Illustrated by Katia Sheremetieva

Dedicated to all incredible grandmas.
We love you very much!

Special thank you to Karine and Elena for being
the best grandmas.

SUGAR

Some grandmas can cook
Some grandmas can read a book
Some grandmas can bake for a whole troupe!

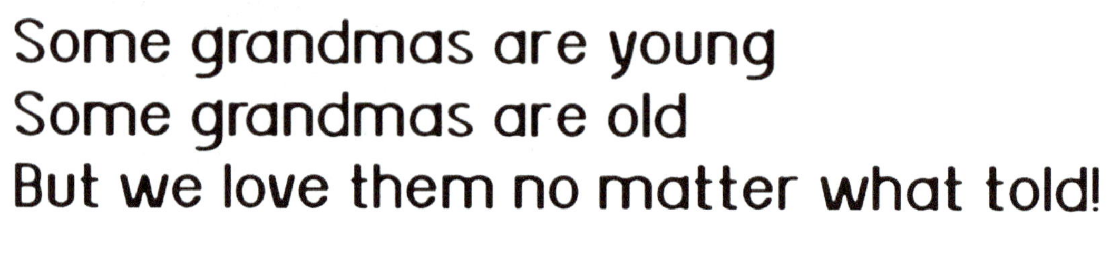

Some grandmas are young
Some grandmas are old
But we love them no matter what told!

Some grandmas love fashion
Some grandmas love their profession
Some grandmas have hair that look like ashen!

Some grandmas are short
Some grandmas are tall
But we need them big or small!

AKERY
OPEN

Some grandmas have work
Some grandmas have pension
Some grandmas do not want to deal with
all that tension!

Some grandmas like puppies
Some grandmas like cats
Some grandmas would rather collect hats!

Some grandmas like forest
Some grandmas like sea
Some grandmas will always drink a cup of tea!

Some grandmas will watch the baby all day
Some grandmas will come for the night and stay

They know how being a mother is
All grandmas do the best there is!

All grandmas are kind
All grandmas are sweet
And without them the life would not be complete

We love our grandmas and respect their time
We know they will always be there full time

We know they are busy and know they are smart
And know that the grandma will always love us by heart!

In loving memories of grandma Masha who knitted the warmest socks on the whole planet.

And to grandma Anya who baked the best pirozhki with cabbage.

You will always be remembered.

www.ingramcontent.com/pod-product-compliance
Lightning Source LLC
Chambersburg PA
CBHW041421300726
48981CB00007B/367